ÁTHA CL

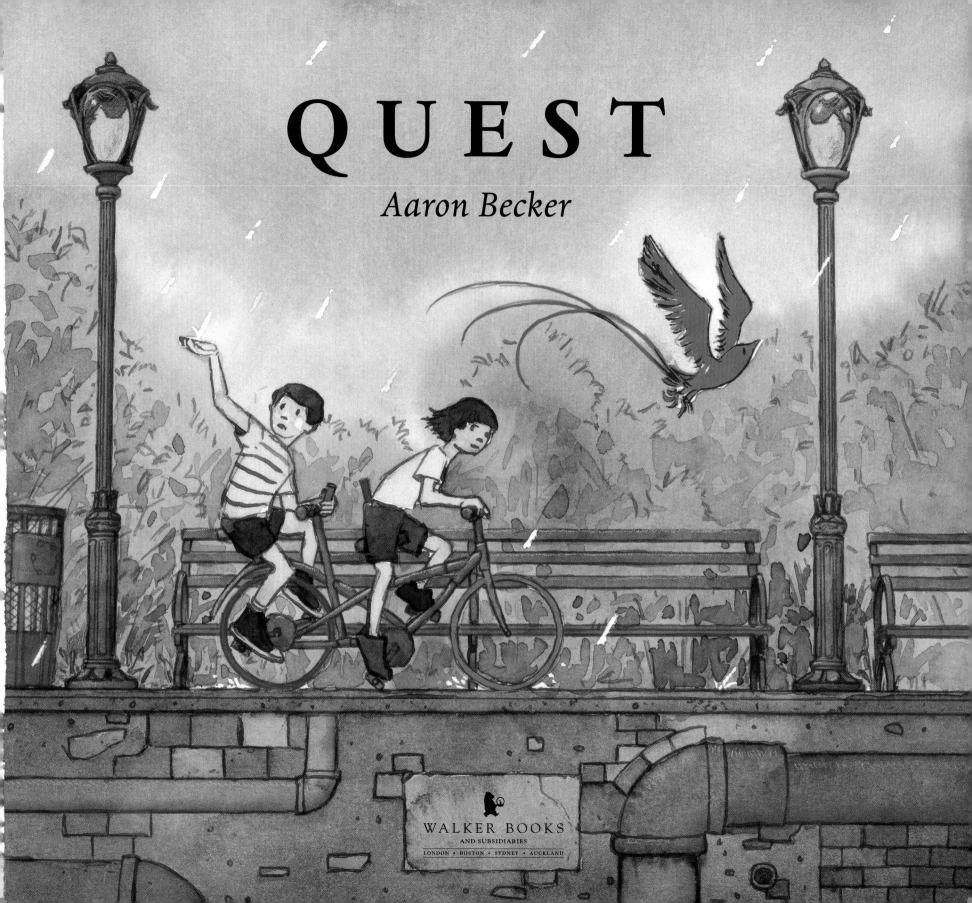

QUEST

Aaron Becker

WALKER BOOKS
AND SUBSIDIARIES

LONDON · BOSTON · SYDNEY · AUCKLAND

For Darci

First published 2014 by Walker Books Ltd
87 Vauxhall Walk, London SE11 5HJ

10 9 8 7 6 5 4 3 2 1

Printed in China

British Library Cataloguing in Publication Data: a catalogue record for this
book is available from the British Library

ISBN 978-1-4063-5766-0

www.walker.co.uk